Sleepover

ILLUSTRATED BY JESS STOCKHAM

Child's Play (International) Ltd

Swindon   Auburn ME   Sydney

© 2009 Child's Play (International) Ltd   Printed in China

ISBN 978-1-84643-280-4

1 3 5 7 9 10 8 6 4 2

www.childs-play.com

Have you packed your PJ's? And a book?

Rabbit's too big. I'll squeeze him in!

This is a big seat! What can you see?

Look at all the shops. Are those potatoes?

It's up these stairs. Look at that *bike!*

Hello! Good trip? It's lovely to see you.

I like your bed. Can I sleep on the top bunk?

Say Hello, Rabbit! Say Hello, Dolly!

What's this? Don't touch! It's not a toy!

What's its name? How fast can it swim?

Help yourselves, everyone. Mmm, yummy!

What have you put in your sandwich?

Can I play horses? Stop! Be careful!

Let me find you something else to play with.

You go first! Look at me, look at me!

I'm up here! Can you catch me?

I love bubbles! This sponge smells good!

Watch out! I'm going to splash you!

It's very dark in here! Where's the light?

Nearly time for bed. Just one more story!

This part's funny. You're good at reading.

Night, night! See you in the morning.

We'll come again soon. Can we get a pet?